# Mail Order Bride

## A Bride for William

### Sun River Brides
### Book 7

# Karla Gracey

First Printing, 2016

# Dedication

I dedicate this book to my mother, as she was the one who kept urging me to write, and without her enthusiasm I would never written and published my books.

# Contents

# Chapter One

The gavel fell. It was finally over. Maddy sighed with relief as she left the courthouse for the final time. Everything that happened to her since January seemed unreal. The months had dragged by, every day bringing a new pain, a new humiliation as she had been forced to sit and watch as others decided her fate. But it had been decided, and she was exonerated. Yet as she listed to the catcalls of the apprentice boys, and saw the way her old friends continued to cross the street, or disappear into stores so they did not have to suffer the indignity of conversing with her, she knew that nothing would change. It was too little, too late.

She clambered into the carriage that awaited her, and accepted Papa's kiss on her cheek. "Are you quite well?" he asked, concern in his eyes. "You look so pale. Maybe we could send you to the Spa at Bristol Springs? Or why not at Saratoga? Your Mama says it is just the place."

"Papa, I am quite well, just tired and glad that it is all done. The last place I wish to be is trapped in a Spa with the women who have been gossiping behind my back about all this."

"You have been ever so brave my darling. We shall punish every newspaper and admonish anyone who has sullied your good name."

"Papa, no. I would rather just let it all die down, so I can move on with my life."

"If you insist," he said pompously. Madelaine knew that tone. It meant he would placate her now, but would ignore her wishes completely. But, if it made him feel better to extract revenge on her behalf, then she could do little to stop him. But, she could do something to ease her own burden. It would be the hardest thing she had ever done, harder even than fighting to clear her name had been. But she was determined. She would never again be responsible for hurting her family so badly.

The carriage pulled up, and she ran inside. She could hear Mama weeping in the drawing room, her heavily pregnant sister comforting her. She would let her Papa inform them of the good news. Maddy had grown weary of her mother's fits of the vapors, the constant tears – as if everything was happening to her, and not Madelaine. She had no doubt that Papa would be successful in packing Mama off to the Spa for a month or two. She was never happier than when she had teams of doctors fussing over her. As she raced up the grand staircase, she wondered if she sounded somehow ungrateful to her parents. She did love them both very much, but they could be so very exasperating at times. She envied her sister having escaped their clutches, but she would do the same – even if her method was a little more unorthodox.

A trunk sat at the end of her bed. She emptied it of the piles of bed linens it contained, and began to thrust dresses and skirts, books and papers into it, not caring about being neat and tidy. She just wanted to get away from Boston as quickly as she possibly could. She was tired, and it had been the worst time of her life. The sooner she could put it all behind her the better. "Papa told us you…" her sister cried as she burst into the room, "won."

"Yes," Maddy said turning to face her. She had kept her plans secret, and was not ready for the confrontation about to come.

"You can't just run away, without anywhere to go?" Carolynn said angrily, as she took in the evidence of Maddy's intended flight. "I know you want to hide, to lick your wounds and start again, but where can you go?"

"I don't know," Madelaine said sadly, sinking onto the bed. It felt as if she had deflated, as if all of the fight in her had been used up in the past months and there was nothing left to even keep her breathing. She had endured enough, and the idea of having to face Society as if none of it had happened was simply too much for her. "But Boston will not forget this. Oh, they may pretend that nothing happened, because of who you are, who you are married to, who Father is even. But they will not ever let me be, in their own way."

"I do understand Maddy, but please don't do anything rash. The girls would miss you terribly, and my time with this one is nigh," she stroked her heavily pregnant belly and looked at her sister with hopeful eyes. Madelaine loved her, but was not prepared to allow anyone to emotionally blackmail her into staying. The simple truth was that if she stayed all she would ever have would be her nieces. There would be no dynastic marriage for her now, nor even one with a young man of even moderate means. She would be infamous.

"I love you Caro, but I will not stay – not even for that. I cannot. And I will not bring our family into even further disrepute by doing so. You have all had to bear such scrutiny, such unpleasantness, because of me."

"Not because of you," Caro exploded. "The charges were dropped The proof is there that this was some kind of spurious attempt to discredit our family somehow. They chose you, because you… oh I don't know why they chose you."

"Because they could. They cannot touch any of the rest of you. But, I am different. I stand out. My work with the slum children hasn't exactly endeared me to the great and good of the city."

"I just don't want you to leave us. We love you, and we need you."

"I know. But this will not be their first and only attack at us. If I go, I take away their easiest target. Things will settle down for you all. They would not dare come against any of you. And I want a family and a husband one day. I want a quiet life, where what I do is not front page news and a man who is honest and good."

"There is no such thing," Caro joked weakly.

"There is, just not in our world. I'm not afraid. I shall write often, and you are more than wealthy enough to visit me whenever you wish once I am settled."

"So you do have somewhere to go?"

"Not yet, but I will. I replied to this," she tossed a small pile of newspaper cuttings towards her sister. An advertisement was circled in red on each.

> *A Gentleman of Montana seeks a good woman to correspond with, for the purpose of matrimony. A gentle disposition, good education and a loving heart are all the subscriber desires. He in turn will offer security, a good home and a bright future. All Replies to Box 38, The Matrimonial Times*

"He does not give much away does he," Caro said wryly as she read the first one.

"No, but neither of us ever expected hearts and flowers. We both knew we would make marriages of expedience. I am just taking matters into my own hands, rather than waiting for Papa to find some horribly ambitious fool, who might be prepared to take me. As you can see, his was not the only advertisement I responded to, but it was as good an example as any."

"Oh Maddy, any man would be blessed to have you as his wife."

"I know, but my character and my abilities will never again be a part of the reasons why any man here would ever consider wedding me. I have to make my own luck now."

Carolynn looked so sad. Madelaine wanted to reassure her that everything would be fine, but everything had changed for her now and she had to face that. Her sister's happiness had been secondary to the benefits both Papa and her husband, Blake, had gained from the union. She had brought him an old family name, and immediate entry into the highest echelons of East Coast Society. He had brought money, and a mercantile enterprise that had gone from strength to strength because of the merging of the two families. But, Caro had been blessed in that she had fallen madly in love with her betrothed, and he with her. They were an indomitable force, and their futures looked bright, as long as no further scandals were linked to them. It did not take much for Boston's elite to turn on you, and older and wealthier families than their own had been ruined before and would be again. But, it would not be over her, not if she could help it.

The scandals that had been linked to her name in recent months had threatened to ruin everything, Maddy was wise enough to know that. The flurry of gentleman callers had stopped almost overnight, the possible match between herself and one of the wealthiest bankers in Boston had vanished as if he had not been courting her assiduously for months. But she did not mind any of that. She did not want some preening peacock, who believed what he read in the newspapers and did not have the courage to ask her what was true. But she did not wish to become a lingering embarrassment to her family either. It would be best for everyone if she were to vanish quietly, never to return and so she had made her preparations, ready for when she found the right man.

"But, if you are still waiting to hear from them, however many of them you wrote to, why must you leave now?"

"Because if I don't I will burst!" Maddy exclaimed. "I have been kept, pent up inside this house for months. My only contact with the outside world has been within a courtroom. I am sick of the sight of everything within these walls. I am sick of the jibes, the snide comments everywhere I go. Even walking from the door to our carriage I have heard the whispers, and even worse at times. One lad called out the most obscene things to me. I am tired of being brave. I cannot pin a smile to my face any longer. I just wish to be somewhere, anywhere, where nobody knows me, or my family, our history. I need to get away before I go mad Caro, can you not even try to understand that?" Her sister sat quietly for a moment, then pulled her in close.

"I do understand. I am sorry, I am being selfish. I had not considered the torment you have been through, or that will continue to be flung at you even though it has been proven to be untrue. I just cannot bear the thought of you being far from me."

"I know. But I shall write, every day if you wish me to. I shall want to know all your news. I love you Caro and I will miss you."

"But you have to go and find a new life, one you can live freely and fully." They clasped each other tightly, tears pouring down both their cheeks.

Once Carolynn had left her, Maddy collapsed onto the bed, sobbing into her pillows. She did not want to leave her family, she loved them all so very much even when they were being infuriating, but the pain she felt every day, the shame and fear she felt when even walking outside of their elegant townhouse was enough to propel her forwards. This was not the way she wished to live her life. She wanted to be back with the children, teaching them their letters and helping them to learn the skills that would help them to escape their poverty and misery. She longed to be assisting gentle Doctor Hailey as he administered to the sick, but she could not do any of that any more.

She gazed down at the pile of advertisements. She had been responding to them for so long. She was beginning to give up hope that anyone would ever write back. Maybe the scandal had made its way out of Boston, and now no man anywhere would consider her? But, as she re-read the words of the Gentleman of Montana she allowed herself to dream. She had only written to him a few weeks ago. He should have received her letter by now. She would have to wait a little while to hear from him, but she still held onto hope that this time she would find the man she needed to save her from her misery.

She pictured him as a rugged type, most at home on the land. His Stetson perched forward to shield his eyes from the sun, a well-bred stallion between his strong thighs. Out on the land from sun up to sun down, he was tanned and lean. But, she also pictured him sat by the fire, reading a book or showing his children how to form their letters. Their home was not luxurious, certainly nothing like the home she had lived in her entire life, but it had everything they needed, and was cozy and warm.

She had added a few touches to make it more homely, and they were well liked by everyone nearby. She taught Sunday School and helped the local doctor with his rounds when their two boys were in school.

It was a lovely picture, but it was becoming more and more faded as time went on. Each man who did not respond to her correspondence broke her heart just a little more, making her wonder what her options might be if she could not secure herself a husband. She could always become a governess, but nobody on the East Coast would hire her to care for their children, and she wasn't sure if she had the courage to head West alone.

# Chapter Two

His office was full. William Butler wasn't sure if he should be happy about it or not. That the people of Sun River had grown to trust him and sought him out to tend to their needs was a good thing, but that there were so many people in need of his medical expertise was not. He called in his first patient of the day, and settled in to the routine of stomach aches, ear and throat infections and other minor ailments that plagued the townsfolk. He teased the children gently, coaxed their Mama's into agreeing to give them more regular baths, and tried to find ways to make vegetables more appealing. But, every day they fought him. He smiled as he thought of the multitude of disgusted faces he was privy to when he dispensed his wisdom, but he persevered.

So much of the illness he saw could be prevented with such simple measures, he was convinced of it. He spent much of his free time poring over the new studies that were being published about hygiene and the differences in health outcomes between the rich and poor. He was convinced that the biggest difference between rich and poor was in the food they ate. Rich people ate a broader range of foods, and considerably more fruits and vegetables and they most definitely suffered from less petty health concerns. He wondered if there was a way to prove his theories, but as a small town doctor he did not have the resources to do such a thing. He was sure though that there were ways in which he could encourage people to take care of themselves better, and he hoped that there were people within the community now that he could convince to assist him. He knew that both Catherine and Myra would be glad to help with the children, but their parents would be harder to convince.

"Doctor Butler?" He looked up. Tom stood in his doorway, waiting politely to be invited in.

"Come in, what ails you my friend?" he asked.

"Nothing Will. I brought your post – and wondered if you would care to join us for supper tonight?"

"Thank you, that is kind of you – on both counts!" Will grinned.

"Catherine would like to discuss your ideas for teaching the children how to grow things more, and I am glad to be of assistance." The two men smiled at one another. Will had been at Tom's side as he tried to banish his troubles with alcohol. They had built a close friendship, and their combined experiences in that field had helped when Catherine's Father had come to stay in order to give up his own demons. They had waved the old man off on the train, back to Boston, just a few days ago and were hopeful that he had the strength to resist now, even when back in his old life.

"How is she, now that Nathaniel has gone home?"

"Concerned I think. She has been throwing herself into every project that comes her way. Until she has regular reports that he truly is doing well, I think she will find it hard not to be."

"I have referred him to an old friend of mine. He is an excellent physician, and a good man. I am sure Nathaniel will find him good to confide in."

"Thank you for that, I know she appreciates it."

"So, what time should I come?"

"Around seven?"

"And who is in charge of the Saloon?"

"Ethan. He is a good man, and a good bar tender. I look forward to seeing you tonight, Doctor," he said as he dropped the letters on the desk and made his way out.

"Indeed," Will said, staring at the pile of envelopes. Three bore the return address of the Matrimonial Times, and he sighed. He had hoped there might be more. So many of his friends in Sun River had made successful matches by placing advertisements in the press and he longed to emulate their happiness. He wasn't sure how many responses any of them had gotten, but the women they had chosen all seemed to have been perfectly suited to them. He had pondered long and hard before he had chosen to follow their lead, but he still had doubts that it would be possible to find the perfect woman in such a calculated manner. But, he did not have time to open them now. He had a waiting room full of people, and so his own future would just have to wait a little longer.

Finally his day was done, and he made his way upstairs to his tiny apartment. He lit a fire, and washed himself carefully. After putting on a clean shirt, he sank into his chair and opened the first of the letters.

*Dear Gentleman of Montana,*

*Firstly, I would like to say that I hope that this letter finds you well. There has been the most horrible outbreak of diphtheria in the tenements and slums here in Boston. I work there when I can, and so every time there is some kind of issue there I worry about everyone I know, and even those I do not.*

*I would very much like to hear about the bright future you plan for yourself, and your bride-to-be. It must be wonderful to hold your destiny in your own hands, knowing you have a good home and the security upon which you may build. I would very much like to hear about your work, and about you. I picture you as a rugged mountain man, though I am sure that the truth is probably much less romantic! I do so hope you won't mind my imaginative tendencies.*

*I was not entirely sure what kind of a woman you were*

praying might respond to you, but hope that I will suit. I am lucky enough to have a fine education. My Father is quite wealthy, and therefore I had the finest governesses, and tutors his money could buy. As all young ladies are, I am also able to draw and paint, play the pianoforte and to sing. I find these pursuits can be most soothing, especially when my work has been hard. But, I would gladly give them up, if required. I appreciate that not everyone can afford the time for hobbies.

I do not highlight my abilities and extreme good fortune in order to crow, or boast. I wish to leave my privileged life behind me forever, should I be lucky enough that you choose me to correspond with, and hopefully in the fullness of time to become your wife. I mention it, because it was one of your few stipulations, that respondents be educated. I am.

I have also been told that I am good hearted. As I mentioned above, I often work in the tenements and slums. I teach the children their letters, and assist a friend of mine who is a doctor to bring them medicines and knowledge on how to care for each other best when sick. My love of such work is frowned upon by many in Society, but I do it because it is so wonderful to see these people's lives change. It is not fair that some have so much, when others have so little, do you not think?

I am never happier than when I am there. I find such joy amongst people who should in all honesty be miserable. Their lives have so little color, or pleasure and yet they find much to celebrate. They love so passionately and fiercely, and truly seem to grasp life in a way those in my own circle do not. I see too much privilege, and it has made people complacent. They believe they deserve such luxury, simply because of their birth. My sister married a merchant, and for some time the match was deemed to be beneath dear Carolynn – but Blake has continued to prove himself, making more and more money and of course that has endeared him to all.

Yet everything feels like a prison. We must act a certain

*way, dress a certain way, follow a calendar of events that never changes. Worst of all is the belief that we must only marry amongst our own. However, I do not wish to make a dynastic marriage. I have no desire at all for such a marriage. I truly wish to wed for love, to have a family and to be my own person. I wish to take my destiny into my own hands, and so I am writing to you. I do hope that I will be considered. I am sure that you will have many responses to peruse, and I understand that I may be waiting some time for a reply – but I pray you will look upon me kindly.*

*Yours With Utmost Hope*

*Madelaine Crane*

Will pondered the heartfelt words. He was unsure. She sounded quite genuine, but he couldn't help but wonder whether a woman of her background could possibly be ready for such a different life. True, he was no rugged mountain man, as she dreamed, nor a rancher or even a farmer. But life as a small town doctor here in Montana was tough. Life for women here in Sun River was not easy. There were risks that even the most prepared of women would struggle to cope with. He put the letter down reluctantly. He couldn't deny there was something about the way she wrote that was truly alluring, a combination of hope and realism that he had not expected.

The other two letters left him feeling more than a little disgusted. Both seemed determined to insist upon their needs, their wants and did not care one jot for his. Neither was suitable, and the way they wrote had been harsh and unfeeling. Their education had taught them the basics, but not any refinement. Yet, Madelaine seemed to be too refined. He did not know what to do. Maybe he should just continue to wait. Hopefully there would be someone more suitable in the next post.

The clock chimed, and he realized he was running late. He grabbed his hat and coat, and for some unknown reason picked up her letter and stuffed it into his pocket as he rushed down to the public stables, where he kept his stallion, Harper. He saddled him up swiftly and galloped out to the lovely home that Tom and Catherine had made for themselves just outside of town. "I am sorry I am late," he said sheepishly as Catherine gave him a peck on the cheek in welcome.

"That is not a problem in this house," she chuckled. "I don't think Tom has ever been on time for anything in his life."

"Unfair my love," Tom said as he came through from the kitchen and shook Will's hand warmly. "I was on time for our wedding. You were the one who was late for that!"

"That is a bride's prerogative," Will said. They all laughed.

"I am so glad you could come. Tom let slip you had some letters from a certain newspaper," Catherine probed gently. Tom looked at her as if he could murder her on the spot. "Oh don't be a ninny, nothing stays secret in Sun River for long."

"So it would seem. I am not ashamed. It would be foolish to be so when so many men in town have found wives that way."

"That is true," Tom admitted. "So, did anyone make your heart pound?"

"It is only a first letter," Will said.

"I knew from the first," Catherine said dreamily.

"Me too," Tom admitted. "There was just something about the way Catherine wrote that just let me know it was her."

Will thought for a moment, unsure if he should tell them of Madelaine. He still wasn't sure about her himself, but like Tom had found, there was definitely something about the way she wrote that made her intriguing. "Will you read this for me?" he finally asked them as he pulled out her letter from his pocket. Catherine nodded, her face serious.

"Are you truly sure? This is something only you can decide."

"I know, and yes I am. There are just a few things, I just want to know if you see them too."

Catherine took the paper and began to read. Tom perched on the chair beside her, reading over her shoulder. The room was quiet, but not silent. Will could hear the gentle ticking of the clock, and even the in and out of their breath.

"You are worried about her coming from a wealthy background?"

Catherine asked perceptively. "You like her, but fear she will not be able to fathom the dangers and difficulties here?" He nodded. There was little point in denying it. Tom simply laughed. Will looked at him, shocked.

"What?" he asked.

"You do know that Catherine was a Parker, do you not? I mean, you do know that Nathaniel was once one of the wealthiest men in America?"

"No I did not," Will admitted. "I never asked for his surname. He was introduced to me as Nathaniel, and I don't know why but I never asked for more than that!"

"So, do you think that I am unable to cope out here alone, should anything ever happen to Tom?" Catherine asked him.

"I would never be so foolish. You are more than a match for him."

"Then I think that if you like everything else you should find out more. She is already less sheltered than I was, has spent time working in the slums. She understands hardship."

"Did you know her?"

"No, the Crane's moved in circles way above ours. We probably would have known them once. I could ask Papa if he does – men seem to be much less rigid about these things. But, we weren't moving in the more elevated echelons of society after Mama died. First we were in mourning, and then Papa had begun to drink and gamble and we slipped slowly downwards. Standards had to be maintained, but the Cranes moved to Boston from New York once we were out of favor."

Will tucked the letter back in his breast pocket, close to his heart. He had much to think on, but Catherine was probably right. Women were so much stronger than men ever gave them credit for. He would not hesitate to place his trust and faith in any of the women he knew here in Sun River. That Catherine had enjoyed a similar upbringing, protected and sheltered, and yet was the indomitable force that he knew definitely made him reconsider his earlier thoughts. Then he thought of Maggie, Alice and Ellen, all women who had worked, but had lived in Boston their whole lives; Myra and Annie who had been in service; and even Emily who had travelled the country in the circus as a child, and settled in Boston. The city seemed to have influenced them all, and all were women he admired and would be honored to call his wife.

# Chapter Three

Maddy made her way to the postal office every day. She had not wanted her family to know her business, and now with Caro constantly filling her with horror stories of what could go wrong she wished she had maintained her silence. But, every day there was no reply and she felt just a little bit more desperate. She simply couldn't stay here in Boston any longer. She would buy herself a train ticket, to the first place she could, if there was no word from him. She would build a life alone if she had to.

"Miss Crane, good morning," the postmaster said brightly. "I believe there is a letter for you this day."

"That is wonderful news," she said as she signed for it. The handwriting on the envelope was scruffy, each line drifted downwards and the letters hard to make out. But strangely it did not put her off. In fact it made her smile, that her Gentleman had been in such a rush to respond, that he hadn't worried about something so irrelevant as ensuring his script was immaculate.

She strolled across the street and entered the park. She could see the usual people, wandering hand in hand, a few gentlemen on horseback, ladies in carriages – all hoping to see and be seen. She snuck away from the paths, and into the carefully manicured woodland. It was peaceful and quiet in here. Nobody would disturb her, and she found an old tree stump to sit on and settled down to try and decipher his words.

*"Dear Miss Crane*

*I cannot tell you what pleasure I felt as I read your letter. Something in it spoke to me, and I was quite unable to dismiss you from my thoughts.*

*I am sorry to upset your fantasy, but I am not a rancher or a farmer. I am a small town doctor, and though I believe my opinion is respected, I do not fit the romantic ideal I know modern novels portray! I have a thriving practice, and I hope one day to build a hospital here, that will serve the entire local region.*

*As you can imagine, knowledge that you already assist a doctor in his rounds, and often in such trying circumstances, filled my heart with happiness. A doctor's wife is as important as any medicine I believe. Their commitment to their husband is almost secondary to their ability to put others ahead of themselves. This is why I required someone with a loving heart. My work often has me out late, and up early. My wife will need to understand this, to not be jealous of the time I am forced to spend away from her. So your having pastimes that you enjoy is a blessing, I will at least know that you can entertain yourself when I am busy!*

*I do not know what else to say, I feel oddly tongue-tied as I write this. What do you ask of a woman who so freely offered up such knowledge of herself? I cannot imagine there is anything much more to say and so, as I am finding this so difficult I think it best we meet, and soon. I am much better at talking in person, and am sure we would find out quickly enough if we will suit. So, I have enclosed a train ticket to Chicago. I have arranged accommodation there, in separate hotels, for us both. I will book tickets to the theatre, and maybe we could go somewhere for supper? I am happy to arrange a chaperone should you require one. Please write to me quickly to let*

*me know you are coming?*
*Yours in abject hope*
*Dr William Butler*

Maddy almost jumped for joy. She would be able to escape Boston, and so soon. The ticket was for Friday! She had barely any time to let him know that she was on her way. She tucked the letter away in her reticule carefully and then hurried back to the postal office. "Do you have paper and an envelope?" she asked the Postmaster. He smiled at her indulgently.

"Your sweetheart?" he enquired. "No, don't tell me. Here, take these." He handed her paper, an envelope and pen and ink. "If you hurry I can send it on its way today."

She didn't think about what she should write, she just scribbled five little words, shoved the paper into the envelope, addressed it hurriedly and then handed it and the pennies required to send it to the kindly Postmaster. "Thank you," she said as she tried to control her breathing. Her chest was heaving, and she felt quite overwrought. "I think I need some air."

Once outside she tried to control herself. This did not mean that he wished to marry her. It was only a meeting, but that he had given her the means to leave Boston, and that it was so soon, meant more to her than she had ever realized it would. Her trunk had been packed now for weeks, she simply needed the encouragement his short letter had offered. She did not care one jot if she did not love him on sight. She only cared that he know that she was everything he had ever wanted when they met. She had to make him marry her and take her home to Sun River. She had never been the most accomplished of flirts, and so she knew she needed help.

Rather than heading home, as she usually did to avoid public scrutiny, she made her way to her sister's imposing mansion. Helden, their butler, opened the door when she knocked. "Miss, what a surprise! Mrs Cavendish was not expecting visitors today I do not think."

"No, she wasn't, and especially not me Helden. But I am sure she won't mind if you show me in, whatever condition she may be in. I am her sister after all." He smiled awkwardly.

"Indeed," he agreed. "She is in her chamber I believe."

"At this time of day?" Maddy looked up at the grand clock above the stairs, it was showing midday. Carolynn was an early riser, was never in bed past nine. It was a standing joke that her servants hated her for it, as it meant they never got a moments peace.

"The last few days she has been feeling a little weary I believe, Miss Madelaine."

"Well, she does not have long before her confinement I suppose. I should think she is entitled to feel a little weary. I shall show myself up."

She ran up the stairs, not caring if anybody thought her a hoyden. Boston's opinion mattered not a jot any more. She would only be here for just a few more days after all. "Caro, darling Caro, he answered!" she cried as she rushed into her sister's rooms. Caro was propped up in bed, cushions all around her. She looked pale, but her face lit up with pleasure as Maddy threw herself into her arms.

"Who wrote? Which one?" she teased.

"The Gentleman of Montana," Maddy cried, over the moon. "He is a doctor, and wishes to meet me. He has sent me a ticket to Chicago, to see if we suit." Caro's face fell just a little. Most people would never have spotted it, but Maddy knew her sister too well.

"When do you leave?"

"Friday." They sat in silence, just holding each other's hands.

"Oh Maddy, I am pleased for you – I am," Caro said eventually "But, I shall miss you terribly."

"I know, and I am so very sorry that I shall not be here to see this one into the world," she caressed her sister's protruding belly. "Are you sure you are quite well? You are never so late abed."

"The doctors are a little concerned, that is all. I am to spend every day in bed until the little one arrives."

"I shall stay if you ask me," Maddy said, feeling terribly guilty. Her sister needed her and she was thinking only of her own needs.

"I shall never ask that of you. I know how hard it is for you, I agree that it is unlikely things will ever change. You have to go. I have to know that you have found your place, your happiness once more."

"Thank you. I shall stay here, help with Mina and Hattie until I leave if you would like?"

"I would like that. I know they are running poor Helden ragged with their tearing around the house like demons!" Maddie patted her sister on the hand.

"I shall go and teach them how it is done properly then," she joked.

"I am sure you will," Caro grinned. "But, if you could at least teach them to do it quietly for the next few days it would be much appreciated."

"Your wish is my command."

Maddy left her sister to rest and made her way to the nursery. Her nieces were terrible tearaways, but she adored them. They both reminded her of herself, though they had Caro's beauty. "Aunt Maddy!" they cried as they rushed to hug her. "Where have you been? It has been forever since we saw you last!"

"I know, and I am sorry for that. I have been like poor old Catpuss over there, curled up by the fire, licking my wounds."

"Catpuss was in a fight, were you in a fight?" they asked curiously.

"Of a sort – but not quite like Catpuss. Mine did not involve scratches and bites, at least not physically."

"But you won didn't you? Catpuss always wins," they said proudly. "He is feared by all the other cats."

"As he should be," Maddy said. "I did win," she said. It was true enough, though it didn't feel that way most of the time. "Now, I shall be staying with you for a couple of days, to help your Mama out."

"How wonderful," Hattie said. "Will you play with us?"

"I will." Maddy was determined to spend as much time as she could with her beloved nieces. She wanted to embed herself in their little memories, so they never forgot her – as she knew she would never forget them. She would miss them terribly, but life was not contained within the walls of this well-appointed nursery, and she could not continue to live only half a life hiding from the world. She had to do this, for herself.

She picked up a story book and began to read to the two girls, who curled up beside her. She looked down into their rapt faces, and wondered what it might be like if she had her own children to read with and play with. She had rarely been envious of Carolynn, but as she thought of the happiness her sister had found with Blake, and that she was mother to these two bright and beautiful girls she couldn't help but feel she was missing out on so much that should be hers. She had never intended to be unmarried, yet for some reason Papa had not once approved of any of the young men who had come calling for her, and she hadn't been much impressed by them either.

As the little girls began to nod off she wondered if she would ever find love. She was more than happy to settle for companionship and was sure that she would find it with Doctor William Butler. They appeared to have much in common, a desire to help others less fortunate than themselves for one. She stroked Hattie's hair and carefully moved Mina's head from her lap and stood up. Whatever it took, she would make this gentleman like her. She was not prepared to wait any longer to have a home and a family, and she couldn't wait to be away from the gossips and the cruelty of the people she had once called her friends. But, more importantly she looked forward to being a doctor's wife. She was sure that together she and William could make a difference to many people's lives, and that together they could build that hospital, and ensure that everyone received the care they needed.

# *Chapter Four*

*I am on my way!*

William looked at the short note again, and grinned, inanely. He couldn't describe the pleasure he felt at the five simple words written in her exquisite script. He tucked it back into his pocket, and looked out of the train carriage window. He loved watching how the terrain changed as he crossed the country, though even as he had barely left them behind he found himself missing the snow-capped mountain peaks of his adopted home. He had not been to Chicago for many years, but he hoped that the city would not have changed too much. He was sure that it would be bigger and busier as most towns and cities seemed to be these days, but he prayed that it would still be welcoming and friendly. He wanted to be able to show Miss Crane a wonderful time, wanted her to be charmed and intrigued about travelling further.

"Excuse me, Sir?" A young woman, with a cheeky looking boy sat opposite him. He was surprised to hear her speak, she had been silent for much of the journey.

"Yes, how can I help?" he asked her.

"I am sorry to be any trouble to you, but I couldn't help but notice you have a doctor's bag with you?"

"Indeed, I am a doctor, is there something wrong?"

"Not with me, but with my boy. The doctor in Great Falls told me he could not help, but that his friend in Chicago might be able to. I don't know, I just don't think Edwin is as sick as the doctor made him out to be, at least not now at any rate. I know I am here, on my way to see this gentleman, but he seems so much better now."

"Did the doctor tell you what he thought was wrong with your boy?" Will asked gently. The woman was clearly upset, and she wouldn't be the first person, nor the last, to be given a wrong diagnosis, and cheated by a man she should be able to trust.

"He didn't give me a name, said it would mean nothing to me and might only worry me. Please, could you examine him for me? Tell me if I am doing the right thing?"

"But, Madam, I could be as much of a fraud as you suspect your own doctor to be," he said with a smile. She looked at him intently.

"I doubt it. I have seen how much you cherish that letter, you seem overcome with happiness whenever you read it. I doubt any man who can feel that much for someone – I presume it is a woman you will be meeting when we arrive in Chicago – could be so cruel as to gull me."

"You would be surprised," Will said wryly. "I once heard of an old colleague of mine, we studied medicine together, he most certainly loved his wife and children – yet he was forced to leave New York because of his mishandling of patient's cases. I am afraid it does happen."

"You are right, I should not be so trusting. But you are the doctor from Sun River are you not?" He nodded. "Then I know that you are as good a man as you are a physician. Your reputation spreads even through the corridors of a railway train! There is always talk in the sleeping cars, and there is many a young woman who would be more than happy for you to cast your eyes her way."

"It is a shame I never met any of them before this," Will joked. "But to business. Tell me about your boy."

The young woman sighed, her relief was palpable. "Well, it started with what I thought was a bad cold. He had watery eyes and his nose was terribly runny. He began to rub at his eyes and they became sore, and red. He could hardly tolerate even the weakest sunlight. He became tired and irritable, and he is usually such a sunny boy."

"Did he ever have any grayish-white spots in his mouth, on his tongue? Any fever?" Will asked. She nodded. "And then a few days later he got a rash?"

"Yes, however did you know?"

"Your son has had measles," he concluded. Her face fell, and Will was quick to reassure her. "Though measles can indeed be fatal, he seems to be lucky that it was not a particularly virulent case. As you say he is healing, and should be quite well again in a week or so. He is obviously a very lucky little boy, and has a particularly strong constitution."

"So the other doctor?"

"I suspect he and his friend have a little scam I'm afraid. They send a boy, who appears to be healing anyway to the second doctor, who claims a miracle cure down to some particular tonic or treatment regimen, and you pay them a large sum of money because you are so grateful your boy did not die."

"But, what if he had gotten worse?"

"Then I am sure that they would have both been very grave, and terribly sympathetic to your loss. My advice to you is to take your boy home. We shall be stopping soon, get the first train back and get him into bed. Keep giving him plenty of fluids, bathe him in lukewarm water, with oats in it to help the itching and in no time he will be his usual sunny self."

"Thank you Doctor, I cannot thank you enough for putting my mind at ease. I know of so many women who have lost their children, I would have done anything to ensure I didn't lose him."

"I think you should find a new doctor." He scribbled the name of another physician in Great Falls that he knew was trustworthy. "I think you will find Doctor Gregson will be much more trustworthy."

"I am so sorry to have troubled you, it is not right of me to have done so – and in a railway carriage of all places. But I cannot thank you enough. How much do I owe you for your time?" she asked pulling out her purse.

"Nothing. It doesn't count unless you are from Sun River," he said with a wink. "I am just glad to have helped. Now, one final thing, the names of the two doctors please? I think I should pay them both a visit, don't you?" She nodded and told him, and as the train pulled into the station he helped her to get her bags ready to disembark. "Get well Edwin, and try not to worry your Mama so!" He ruffled the lad's hair, and the two left him with a wave.

The rest of his journey was thankfully much less eventful, and passed swiftly. He was soon standing on the platform in Chicago, waiting for Miss Crane's train to arrive. The porter at his side was bored, and stood nonchalantly smoking a cigarette as Will paced nervously up and down. Finally the huge locomotive arrived in the station, and once the smog cleared Will went in search of her. But, he could not find a young woman alighting from any of the carriages. He began to panic, maybe something terrible had happened? Maybe she had decided not to come after all? Maybe she had taken one look at him and decided to hide?

"Doctor Butler?" a soft voice said as he felt a light hand tap him on the shoulder. He turned, surprised to find that she was almost as tall as he. He took a step back, as he took in her cascade of long blonde hair, and the elegant outfit she wore with such grace. The blue velvet set off the vivid blue of her eyes, so deep it was almost violet. She was quite beautiful, and he could hardly believe that this young woman was here to meet with him. Surely she should have had hundreds of young Boston men falling at her feet?

"Miss Cccrane?" he stammered, feeling more nervous than he could ever remember.

"Please, do call me Madelaine, or Maddy if you'd prefer."

"Mmmm Maddy. That is lovely. I am so sorry, I do not normally make such a complete fool of myself at first meetings, but I wasn't expecting you to be…"

"So tall? So blonde?" she asked mischievously, her eyes sparkling.

"So beautiful," he admitted. "I do not know why, but the way you write it gave me the impression of someone maybe more handsome, than pretty." He could feel the heat rising up his neck and into his cheeks, knew that he looked and sounded a complete fool. "I am sorry, that sounds as if I believe that an intelligent and eloquent person cannot also be so stunningly lovely. If I ever did, I will never believe so again." She smiled at him again.

"I am so pleased that I am not the only one of us to be nervous about this," she confided. She pulled off her gloves to show him her nails. "See, I have quite bitten my nails to the quick with anxiety!" Unable to stop himself, he took the proffered hands, and kissed each fingertip. Her eyes were wide when he looked back up into them.

"I am too forward. I am sorry. I can arrange a chaperone, do not wish you to ever feel uncomfortable," he said, feeling utterly flustered. She laughed, the tinkling sound was like music, it flowed through him, as life giving and wondrous as water to a man dying of thirst."

"I do not mind one bit, and a chaperone could be so terribly tedious. We are both adults Doctor Butler, shall we not be able to take care of our own interests? I doubt you would ever force yourself upon anyone."

"No I most certainly would not, and please if I am to call you Maddy you must call me Will."

"Will," she said softly. The word seemed to sound completely different in her dulcet tones. "I shall be honored."

She gave him her hand, and he tucked it under his arm, escorting her happily to where a line of carriages awaited. The bored porter scampered along behind them, his trolley now filled with her trunk and his valise. Will tipped him gratefully and assisted Maddy inside. "I have arranged for you to stay at the Great Northern Hotel, and I shall be staying at Tremont House, though if you would prefer we can swap?"

"I do not mind where I sleep, as long as I get to spend as much time as possible with you. We have much to discuss, and I do not want to waste a moment of our time together," she said breathlessly. He had to admit, sitting so close by her in such a confined space was making it hard for him to breathe too, or concentrate on anything other than the sensation of warmth that emanated from her body.

"I have booked us a place for supper at a delightful restaurant, and thought that we could maybe go to the museum tomorrow, and take in a play at the theatre in the evening?"

"That sounds wonderful," she said, not taking her eyes from his. "I am sure that it will all be wonderful."

Will had never believed in love at first sight, yet he had never before met someone like Maddy. Her sheer physical impact was overwhelming. He simply could not understand how she could still be unwed, and how lucky he had been when he had chosen her to write back to. He reminded himself to send Catherine gifts every single day in thanks for her assistance in making up his mind. He was sure he would never regret it.

When they reached her hotel, he was loathe to leave her there alone. "I shall be quite alright," she assured him. "I have faced much worse than the wagging tongues of hotel staff." She laughed, but he was sure he detected a touch of strain in her tone. But, she must be tired, he admonished himself. He must not be the doctor here. It was not his place to analyze every symptom as if she were a patient, rather than a woman he intended to court. He watched as she and her trunk disappeared up the stairs, and wished he could follow her, but the hansom cab was waiting outside, and he must go and check in to his own rooms if he was to be refreshed and back here to collect her for supper.

As he bathed and dressed for the evening he tried not to read too much into the fact that she had brought such a large trunk with her. He was sure that most women probably travelled with more accoutrements than men, and their dresses must take up considerable room with all the petticoats, corsetry and other undergarments women seemed to be so enamored of these days. He was not sure that the fashion for such a tiny waist was altogether healthy. Young women, supposedly in the peak of health should not be so prone to fainting, he was sure.

Maddy was waiting for him in the foyer. She wore a dusky pink gown that had an exquisitely embroidered bodice and full flaring skirts. Her hair was pinned artfully so that it draped over one shoulder in elaborate coil. She looked quite simply magnificent. He quickly asked the bellboy to dismiss the carriage he had waiting outside. He wanted to see and be seen with this beauty by his side. He bowed gallantly to her and offered her his arm. "The evening is fine, would you care for a stroll?" She nodded.

"So, where are you taking me? I hope the food is good – I am absolutely ravenous," she admitted cheekily.

"I should have asked, do you like fish?" he said, suddenly feeling concerned about his choice of restaurant. So many people did not enjoy it, but Rector's was one of his favorite places and he always tried to eat there at least once when he visited Chicago. She gave him a long and serious look, and he began to feel hot under the collar. He ran his finger around it to loosen it a little and even mopped his brow before she put him out of his misery.

"I love it, especially oysters."

"That is wonderful news as we are to go to Rector's Oyster House. They also do the most wonderful cocktails, the concoctions are quite unexpected!" She licked her lips in anticipation, and the simple gesture almost made him lose control and kiss her right there in the middle of the street. But, he pinned his eyes forward, and tried not to think about the light touch of her hand on his arm, or the feel of her hips as they ever so gently swayed against his own.

# Chapter Five

Maddy rolled over in her vast bed as the maid came in with her morning chocolate. She felt quite deliciously decadent, having slept in until almost ten. She was to meet Will at the zoological gardens at midday, so she had time to luxuriate in the pleasure of a real bed and plenty of pillows. The past few days had flown by, too quickly as far as she was concerned. Will would have to return to Sun River tomorrow, and she was still uncertain whether he intended to take her with him. She prayed he would, but he was not an easy man to read. She was certain that he liked her, he enjoyed her company and did not seem to object to her more forcibly expressed opinions as so many men had done in her past. Yet, since that delightful moment at the train station when he had kissed every one of her fingertips he had not made any kind of physical gesture towards her.

She had to admit it was quite frustrating, as she most certainly would not rebuff his advances if he were to try. She had come here, resigned to the thought that she would marry him if he wanted her, that her own feelings for him did not really matter. Yet, from the very first she had been smitten with his deep brown eyes, slightly scruffy and overlong hair, and his tendency to worry about how everyone else around him was feeling. He was quick-witted, and funny yet his humor was self-deprecating and endearing. She wondered if he knew just how good a man he was.

Her breakfast completed, and a delightfully warm bath, scented with rose petals, later and she was ready to join him. She picked up her parasol, as the sun was hot, and walked slowly towards the gardens. A young bellboy from the hotel was her guide, and he delighted in pointing out the kinds of sights that only the young in a city like this ever get to know. She smiled at his eagerness and was happy to give him a dollar for his troubles as they reached the gates. Will was standing, his jacket slung casually over his shoulder, he turned and the glint of his pocket watch in the sun made her blink for a moment. "You look lovely," he said softly as he took her hand.

"Thank you. So, what is on our itinerary today?" she asked, trying to hide the way that his innocent touch was making her feel. Just the sensation of his skin on her own was sending shivers through her, and when he bent to kiss her hand, she gasped as he turned the palm and kissed that, before closing her fingers over the spot, as if sealing it. It was intimate, a lovers kiss. She glanced around, wondering if anyone else had seen the look of pure ecstasy she was sure must have crossed her features. She blushed.

"Well, I have a date with the tigers," he said, innocently as if he had missed every moment of her delight. She wanted to scream out loud, and beg him to see her, truly see her – to see that she was smitten, and longed for him to make her his wife. But she was too well bred, and so she kept her own counsel and tried to reconcile herself to the thought that tomorrow, this wonderful man might just walk out of her life forever.

As always he tucked her arm through his, and escorted her proudly to their destination. A keeper was awaiting them at the enclosure and he gave them the most interesting lecture on the big cats. If she hadn't been so on edge, Maddy would have been utterly entranced, but she could barely drag her attention from the man by her side. "So, shall we go and see our newest acquisition?" the keeper asked. Startled, she looked at him completely confused.

"I'm sorry, I must have lost track. The heat," she said vaguely.

"Mr Moss has a special treat for us," Will said gently, as he urged her forward. Still feeling a little bewildered, she followed the stocky little keeper inside a nearby building. Inside she could see the cages that the beasts slept in at night. It was fascinating, and she could hardly believe her luck, that Will had arranged something so wonderful for her.

"This is Tilly," Mr Moss said proudly as he stopped at a cage that seemed to have no access to the outside pen. "Isn't she beautiful?" Maddy moved to his side and looked down, looking up at her was a tiger cub, with the biggest eyes she had ever seen.

"Oh my," she gasped. Will moved up close beside her, slipping his arm around her waist.

"Isn't she wonderful? Just look at the size of her paws!"

"Would you like to go in? She is due for her feed," Mr Moss asked. Maddy was stunned. Surely this was a wild animal, they should not be allowed even near to her. "Don't worry, she is quite harmless, is more than used to us keepers. Thinks I am her Mama!"

"She will let me feed her?"

"I think she would be more than happy to. Oh, and she likes having her nose scratched while she eats," he added. Will grinned at her as Mr Moss led her into the enclosure. She looked at him, trepidation being outdone by excitement and interest as she knelt down and took the bottle and offered it to Tilly.

The little cub took it happily, clearly not worried in the slightest who was holding it. Mr Moss indicated that she should sit down on a box he brought her, and she did, her skirts spreading around her. Tilly lapped at her milk, occasionally batting at the bottle with her paws. She was strong, but gentle, and her claws were tightly sheathed. Soon she was climbing up into Maddy's lap, and she was able to stroke her nose as Mr Moss had told her to do. It was soft and furry, like velvet. The cub chuffed gently in pleasure as she lay sated on Maddy's lap, her bottle finished

It was magical; she could have cried it was such an incredible thing to have been able to experience. Whatever happened between herself and Will, she would never ever forget this – nor anything else they had enjoyed together over the past few days. He had gone out of his way to make every moment special, and she was overwhelmed by his generosity.

"We should leave her to sleep now," Mr Moss said as he gently eased the young cub from Maddy's lap and settled her into her straw bed.

"Thank you, for everything," Maddy said ecstatically as they parted company with the kindly keeper, and let him go about his duties.

"It was my pleasure. Take care Will, best of luck," he said enigmatically.

She and Will began to walk back through the park. "I have a feeling you know Mr Moss quite well," she said to him.

"Indeed. He is my cousin," Will admitted. "He was more than happy to do me a favor when I told him why I needed it."

"And why was that?"

"Well, I have something to ask you, and I wanted to ensure you were in the best mood I could possibly manage."

"That sounds quite ominous," Maddy said with a rueful smile.

"I shall just come out and say it," he said, fidgeting with his pocket watch, and barely meeting her eyes. She began to feel her fear rise once more, that he would not want her to accompany him back to Sun River - that all this had just been to make her trip worthwhile.

"Then do," she said impatiently.

"Maddy, darling Maddy, will you marry me? I adore you, and want to spend the rest of my life with you!" he gushed.

Maddy could hardly believe her ears, he was saying everything she had been dreaming of, even before she had known how much she loved him, yet for some reason she could not answer. Her words got tangled up in her throat, and she found herself gasping for breath. "Maddy, please are you quite well?" he asked anxiously. "I would never have asked you if I did not think that you cared for me too. Please tell me I have not been a complete fool?"

"No, you have not. Could never be," she finally managed to force out. "Will, I would be honored to marry you, cannot think of anything I could ever want more."

She had barely caught her breath when he picked her up and whirled her around, clearly not caring for the stares of passing strangers. His face was alight with joy, and she could feel tears pricking in the back of her eyes as a lump formed in her throat. It had been so long since she had caused anyone to be so happy, and all because of her. "Shall we go and find a minister right now?" he asked her eagerly. "I do not wish to hurry you, but I cannot bear the thought of having to part with you, want you to come home with me tomorrow and do not wish to do anything to sully your reputation before I whisk you away."

He set her down, and Maddy felt every bit of joy ebb from her body. He could never ruin her reputation, it was already in tatters and he did not know. She had not mentioned her reasons for searching for a husband once since they had met. She suddenly felt as if she had been lying to him, had been leading him on. Yet, she truly did adore him. She wished to be his wife because of that love, no longer because he was the answer to her dilemma. She could not continue to take advantage of this kind and generous man. She had to tell him, but how? It simply wasn't something you could slip into a conversation that easily, and she had no clue as to whether he would understand.

But, could she consider taking the risk that he might never find out? Was that even fair? She wanted to be wed to him so very much, but how could she ever offer herself to him fully knowing of the secret she was keeping from him. News travelled quickly. She did not doubt that there was nowhere on earth where her disgrace would not catch up with her. But, was she selfish enough to take the happiness he was offering her now, and let what would come occur in its own time?

"Maddy? Whatever is the matter?" Will asked, concern written all over his face. "You have gone as white as a sheet! I shall escort you to the hotel immediately, you must rest. I shall send word of the arrangements for our marriage, if that is still what you wish?" She nodded, unable to speak – too scared of what she might say. "Come my darling, it is just the sun and the excitement that has left you overwrought. I cannot tell you how happy you have made me." His words did nothing to assuage her guilt, only made it harder for her to ever admit the truth of her past, and her flight from Boston. But would he ever understand? Would any man?

# Chapter Six

Will sat nervously in his hotel room. He had found a Methodist minister happy to marry them that very evening, but he was concerned as to whether Maddy was well enough. She had seemed to be so happy, and then it was as if all the blood in her body had disappeared. He had been impressed, thus far, with her ability to keep up with him as he had set them a punishing schedule of sightseeing and activity. Clearly it had all been too much for her. He wondered if he would be able to prolong his stay a little, to give her time to rest before they made their way back to Sun River, but he knew it would be impossible. He had already left his patients without a doctor for too long, and did not want to be responsible for anyone dying because of a lack of care.

The clock ticked slowly, and he did not know if he was anxious about waiting for the ceremony, or if he expected her to send him notice that she would not be attending. She had seemed so over the moon at his proposal, and then so utterly dejected. He wondered if there was something in her past that had given her pause, but she didn't talk of her family or her life in Boston and so he had no clue if it might be that, or if she had simply not known how to tell him that she did not wish to be his wife.

Unable to bear the silence, he grabbed his jacket and made his way downstairs to the bar. He ordered a single shot of whiskey for his nerves. He nursed it tentatively. He wasn't one for alcohol usually, but each sip seemed to help as it burnt its way down his throat and warmed his chest. "Newspaper?" the bar tender asked him, brandishing a copy of one of the newspapers from New York. He took it; it would help to pass the time. He looked up at the ornate clock above the bar and sighed. Two hours and thirty seven minutes. He began to read. It amused him that so many of the stories revolved around money and politics. Everything in the East did. He was glad he had made his way West once he had completed his medical training. The vacuous and vain people of his acquaintance in New York had never been to his taste.

He skipped past the classifieds section, smiling at the pages of Matrimonial advertisements. Secretly he wished them all the luck that he had been blessed with, that their unions would be as happy as he knew his would be with Maddy. He had advertised looking for companionship, but he was sure that he had found in the elegant Bostonian a true partner, a woman who he could love and who would love him in return. She was just so honest and straightforward – attributes he had rarely assigned to such women in the past.

He began to read through the pages of news from around the country. Various new laws were being proclaimed in Virginia, and there had been a series of murders in Washington. He applauded the former, and was aghast at the details of the latter, but it seemed that the authorities had managed to capture the culprit. The next story was concerning a trial in Boston. A young woman had been fighting to gain her release from a mental institution, having been incarcerated against her will for being attracted to other women. The woman had claimed that it simply was not true, and her husband and family had stood beside her throughout the trial. Thankfully for her she had been released, but the newspaper details were lurid and clearly designed to stir up public sentiment.

Will read them, and felt his own anger rising. The poor woman had done nothing wrong, and even if the allegations had been true it was hardly as if her preferring the company of women to men was such a seditious thing. He knew he was a tolerant man, that many were not so liberal in their views, but even as a doctor he did not understand the idea that to be attracted to someone of the same sex as yourself was a medical issue. No amount of counseling or medication seemed to ever make a bit of difference in such cases, though many of his peers claimed to be able to cure both men and women of such ailments.

But then he stopped. The story continued with the details of the woman she was supposed to have been intimate with, who had not been institutionalized. The insinuation of the article was that this was because of her family connections and wealth, but Miss Madelaine Crane had also testified at the trial, and had vowed under oath that she and the accused had never shared such carnal relations as was alleged. Will's heart stopped. His brain suddenly went into turmoil, and he found himself gasping for air. Why had she not told him of this? Did she think that he would not understand? Was this why she was so eager to meet with him, to wed him?

He glanced back at the page. Both women had been exonerated, and the courts had insisted that the press be fair and impartial when reporting the case, but all Will could see was the sensationalism of speculation in the journalist's summation. He all but spelled it out that he thought that both women were guilty as charged, and that a terrible injustice had been done. While Will could condemn his opinions, and even his prejudices, the entire case left him with too many questions, and he knew he had to see Madelaine before they were to meet at the chapel. He could not marry her if she did not care for him as he did for her, would not marry her if she was prepared to lie to him about something so very important.

He rushed to her hotel, and ran up the stairs to her room. "Sir, you cannot just enter a guest's rooms without us announcing you," the manager cried, puffing and panting as he chased after Will.

"Sir, the woman in question will be my wife in one hour. I have every right to enter her chambers," Will said firmly.

"Sir, please. It isn't seemly. You are not yet wed! This establishment has a reputation, please do not tarnish that."

"Who is here to see me, and who knows my business?" Will retorted, his patience frayed. The door opened, and Maddy stood there, a filmy robe over her shift. Will felt his body react, as it always did to the sight of her, but he could not let his passion get in the way now.

"Mr Marchant, it is quite alright. Come in Will," she said standing aside so he could enter the room. "I shall be checking out shortly anyway. We have no desire to sully the reputation of your hotel."

Will watched her carefully. She was so calm. But, then she did not know why he had come tearing across town. He wondered if she would still be so in control when he told her that he knew all about why she was here, that her wonderful acting skills would do her no favors any longer.

Mr Marchant retreated and she shut the door and turned to face him. "I can see by your face that something is the matter William, so please do share it with me," she said, her voice quavering a little as she did so.

"Is there not something you should have shared with me, before you allowed me to propose marriage?" he asked angrily.

"Yes," she admitted frankly. Her candor surprised him. He had expected her to try and deny everything, to claim that nothing but love had brought her here. "I should have mentioned it to you long ago, but it was one of those things that seemed just too difficult to drop into polite conversation."

"I read about the court case in the newspaper Miss Crane. It is not something one wishes to find out about their fiancée from an external source – especially one so damn biased!"

"Yes the press did rather enjoy making it all out to be so much more sensational than it truly was," she admitted. "Unfortunately everybody in Boston took their word as truth, rather than the ruling of the court. But, I cannot change other people's opinions. I can only hold on to what I know was the truth."

"And that was?" Will said coldly.

"Francesca is a qualified lawyer. She has been my friend for as long as I can remember. We have worked together on a number of charities, and she has often undertaken work for them when legal assistance was required. She always had to get a friend to undertake her court requirements as judges are still reluctant to let women argue motions and fulfill the role completely, but she was getting under the skin of the establishment. She is very talented, but she crossed one too many of the people that matter. A suit she was working on accused one of Boston's finest and he was not happy about it – especially when he lost the case. He blamed her, rather than taking responsibility for his own wrongdoing."

"And so he came up with a charge of lesbianism? It seems rather absurd."

"It was. But he had already tried everything else. It was the only charge his lawyers could come up with in the end that did not need proof. It is very easy to have someone committed to a mental institution, and almost impossible for them to obtain their own release."

"You seem very knowledgeable about it all," Will said bitterly.

"Francesca was my friend. Is my friend. I was in court, to support her every single day. Thankfully she had friends who were prepared to risk their careers for her. Most of them left Boston immediately after the trial – none of them will ever be able to practice law there again I am sure."

"But why were you named?"

"Your guess is as good as mine. Maybe Granville Healy wished to ruin my Father for some reason, or my brother-in-law Blake. Either would make sense as their companies are in direct competition. But it was because I was there. I spent a lot of time, with my friend. We were close, we were often seen embracing in public – not anything untoward of course – but we were as close as sisters. I was easy, and my family connections would mean that I could not be touched. Healy could cause a scandal that would be enough to cause my family problems, but would be unlikely to face any kind of legal fallout from it himself."

"So, why did you stay and stand by her side? Surely that must have only fuelled the rumors?"

"William, I think I know you well enough to know that you would stand by a friend in need, that you would stand up for what is right? Please do tell me if I am wrong, for it is something that could definitely affect my reasons for marrying you."

"Of course I would. My honor would demand I do what is right – not what is easy," he said staunchly. But, he was a man. It was different. She could have saved herself and her family such trouble if she had simply kept out of the way.

"Why should a woman feel any differently?" she asked, as if she was reading his mind. "I could not have stood by and let anything happen to Francesca, could not let such a ridiculous lie tarnish my own reputation, and ruin her life?"

Will sank down onto the bed. He perched there, his hands balled into fists. The entire situation was so wrong. Yet, Maddy seemed so in control and so resigned to what had occurred. "Was it why you wanted to marry me?"

"Oh, dear Will," she said as she sank down to the floor in front of him. "When I responded to those advertisements I just wanted a way out, to get away from Boston. So, yes in a way it is. But that wasn't why I said yes this afternoon."

"I don't understand," he said looking down into her beautiful face. He reached out and stroked her cheek. The skin was so smooth.

"I came here because I needed to get away from the scandal, the gossip. But I fell in love with William Butler once I was here. I know everyone will tell us it is too soon. How can I know how I feel after just a few days? But I do. I loved you from the first; that stilted advertisement and your curt little letter. I longed to be with you, to have you do to me all the things a husband does to his wife from the moment you kissed every one of my fingertips at the station. And when you arranged for me to pet and feed that tiger cub, I knew I would walk on water for you if you asked me."

"So why could you not trust me? Why did I have to learn about your past from a newspaper?"

"Will, seriously? You have told me everything there is to know about your past? Good and bad?" she asked curiously.

"I suppose not, but anything bad in my past was a minor misdemeanor, at worst an indiscretion!"

"And mine was unfounded, speculative gossip. I did not do the things that Francesca and I were accused of having done. I have had to fight for months to clear both our names of such slander – only to find that no matter what we do, it will follow us everywhere we go. Even to this very room." She turned her head from him sadly, as if she had hoped for better from him. She was right to have done so, and Will knew himself to be the one at fault. He could not blame her for wanting to put aside such things, that were obviously still so very painful for her.

"I am so sorry," he said taking her chin and turning her face to his. "I should have had faith in you. I was just so very afraid that it might be true. That you could never love me as I love you. That your heart belonged to her, that I would never be enough for you." She laughed awkwardly.

"Oh dear Will, there has never been anyone in my heart until I met you. You have no competition." He sighed, her words acted as balm to his wounded pride and he bent his head and claimed her lips tenderly.

"Can you ever forgive me for my jealousy and mistrust?"

"Always, but on one condition," she said as her fingers entwined in the hair at his nape.

"Always do what you have done now. If you have questions, queries, doubts – come to me, talk to me, trust me."

"I swear," he said as he pulled her into his arms and kissed her passionately.

# *Epilogue*

The little church in Sun River was full to bursting. Will smiled at his friends and took comfort from the presence of Tom standing by his side. "What made you choose to wait until you were here?" he asked quietly. "Remember you cannot lie, you are in the house of God!"

"We missed our date with the minister," Will said with a grin, as he remembered the passionate argument and even more passionate reconciliation that had followed it.

"So not only did you travel alone with your intended, you took advantage of her innocence too?" Tom teased.

"Not at all. She just decided that she didn't really have a reputation that could be sullied, and took advantage of mine!"

"Phew, you have a firecracker on your hands Will that is for sure."

"I know, and I am more than glad of it. Life will never be dull with Maddy in my life."

The organ struck a chord, and then began to play a wedding march. Will turned to watch his bride make her way down the aisle towards him. He had been so sure of her presence that he had felt no fear.

But as she approached him he felt his stomach begin to churn as the butterflies began to fly. She looked stunning, in her traditional blue gown. He had wanted her to wear the more fashionable white, but she had insisted that she wished their life to be without such artifice. Her Father was by her side, looking proud and he was glad that they had waited. It had been more than difficult to do so, he had found it harder with each passing day to resist Maddy's many charms -but this special day, surrounded by everyone they loved had been worth the wait.

Her sister, Carolynn sat surrounded by her young children, her handsome husband, Blake, by her side. She held their infant son, whilst the girls clambered all over their Papa. It was delightful to see such a loving and happy family. But, he was sad that there were so few faces on her side of the church. Few of her friends had made the journey from Boston, but as she had admitted she wasn't sure that she had ever really had true friends until she came to Sun River. He was touched that some of his friends had chosen to sit on her side, to offer her their support on this important day.

As she reached the altar, he stepped down to take her hand. A young woman he had not yet met smiled at him as he approached and took Maddy's bouquet of wild flowers, and pulled back the long veil that hid her luscious lips and wide violet eyes from his view. He could only presume that this was Francesca, her best friend. Of all the people who had said they intended to attend he had been most nervous about meeting her. He was still a little uncomfortable and angry too when he thought of what had happened to the two women. But, his fears disappeared when he saw the warmth in her eyes, and he looked forward to being able to get to know her better in the days to follow.

Will took Maddy's hand and they turned to the Minister. He couldn't remove the smile from his face as they listened to his homily, and he was happy to see that Maddy seemed to have a permanent look of joy on her face too. The Minister looked at them, pride and contentment on his kindly face. He guided them and spoke the words of the service eloquently in his rich baritone.

"Wilt thou, William Edward Butler have this woman to be thy

wedded wife, to live together in God's holy ordinance in the Holy Estate of Matrimony? Wilt thou love her? Comfort her, honor and keep her in sickness and in health, and forsaking all others keep thee unto her as long as you both shall live?" the minister asked in a loud clear baritone.

"In the name of God, I, William Edward Butler, take you, Madelaine Annabelle Crane to be my wife, to have and to hold from this day forward, for better, for worse, for richer, for poorer, in sickness and in health, to love and to cherish, until we are parted by death; and thereto I pledge thee my troth."

Maddy smiled at him as he spoke the words of his vow, and he knew that he meant every single one of them. He squeezed her hand as she pledged herself to him.

"In the name of God, I, Madelaine Annabelle Crane, take you, William Edward Butler to be my husband, to have and to hold from this day forward, for better, for worse, for richer for poorer, in sickness and in health, to love, honor and obey, until we are parted by death; and thereto I pledge thee my troth."

He kissed his bride, and was overwhelmed as the congregation began to cheer and clap. He wiped a tear from Maddy's eye. "I won't hold you to the obey part," he promised.

"That is good, I am sure I would never be able to abide by it," she said with a grin. They laughed together, and Will knew that their lives together would be full of such moments of happiness and joy.

"So, what do we do now?" he asked her as they made their way out of the church and into the bright sunshine.

"We go to the wedding breakfast that my Papa has so generously paid for. You cannot imagine how happy he was when he found out that the cooks from Young's Hotel lived here in town now. He used to eat there all the time!"

"Ellen and Maggie are rather special," Will admitted. "But I doubt if we will all fit in the bakery," he glanced across the street at the tiny store.

"No, it is at the Saloon," she said with a smile.

"How long do you think we have to stay to be polite?"

"I suppose we should at least stay until after the meal. We will need our strength after all," she said with a flirtatious look in her eyes. Will picked her up and spun her around.

"I love you Mrs Butler."

"I love you too Doctor Butler, but put me down – you'll rumple my dress!"

"Well, we can't have that," he teased as he gently set her down and took her hand, leading her to the Saloon. "Do you truly believe that you can be happy here in this tiny little town? That you won't miss the excitement and drama of Boston?"

"I am happier here than I have ever been Will, I will not desert you – unless I manage to somehow involve myself in another scandal!"

The End

Thank you for reading and supporting my book and I hope you enjoyed it.

Please will you do me a favor and leave a review so I'll know whether you liked it or not, it would be very much appreciated, thank you.

# Other books by Karla

## SUN RIVER BRIDES SERIES

A bride for Carlton #1
A bride for Mackenzie #2
A bride for Ethan #3
A bride for Thomas #4
A bride for Mathew #5
A bride for Daniel #6
A bride for William #7
A bride for Aaron #8
A bride for Gideon #9

## SILVER RIVER BRIDES SERIES

Mail Order Bride Amelia #1

# About Karla Gracey

Karla Gracey was born with a very creative imagination and a love for creating stories that will inspire and warm people's hearts. She has always been attracted to historical romance including mail order bride stories with strong willed women. Her characters are easy to relate to and you feel as if you know them personally. Whether you enjoy action, adventure, romance, mystery, suspense or drama- she makes sure there is something for everyone in her historical romance stories!

CPSIA information can be obtained
at www.ICGtesting.com
Printed in the USA
LVHW092040280321
682767LV00024B/572